Wrath
of the
Siafu
(A Single Link, Book 2)

BALOGUN OJETADE

DEDICATION

I dedicate this book to the strong, Afrikan women warriors who hold it down at home, as well as the battlefield. The powerful mothers, wives, daughters, students, teachers and leaders who have made this earth Heaven for me and countless other men and boys. Heaven is, indeed, a woman.

PRAISE FOR A SINGLE LINK

"Once again, Balogun gives us a book packed with the action, adventure and bits of historical and martial knowledge we've come to know and desire from his books.
It's beautiful to see the essence of a woman captured so brilliantly and without the over-the-top dramatics we usually see when a male author takes on a female character. I came away with a feeling I don't often get, and that was, he understands the female dynamic and the power that exudes from it when a woman has come into the knowledge of herself."

-Yolanda Jacobs, Author / Editor

ACKNOWLEDGMENTS

I would like to acknowledge my readership. You continue to support my work and spread the word about the State of Black Speculative Fiction Movement and the work I do within it. For that, I am eternally grateful!

I would also like to acknowledge Daniel Flores. Your cover artwork is amazing, brother and I look forward to working with you again, soon!

ROUND ONE

Remi circled Eboni, darting from side to side like a mongoose locked in battle with a cobra and seeking an opening in which to strike. They had sparred many times over the past year. Although Remi had retired from professional fighting after defeating Chris Cunningham nearly two years ago, she continued to spar regularly – she had to stay sharp. Her weekly ten rounds with Eboni Ahmed – the undefeated women's champion for six years – helped with that. Eboni was fast, powerful, experienced and was the best student Remi's husband, Kundo, had ever coached.

Well, second *best,* Remi thought.

But today, Eboni seemed, somehow... off. Her timing, usually razor-keen, was dull and her gait was a bit off-balance and heavy. Remi lowered her hands.

"Eboni? Are you okay?"

Eboni pounded her gloved fists together and nodded her head. "I'm good girl, let's go!"

"Eboni," Remi sighed. "Sit down. Let me look at you."

"Girl, you better put your guards up!" Eboni replied. "You were a champion, so I know Kundo taught you better than that. And you know *me*; you know I'll rock you, hands up or not."

"Whatever," Remi said, rolling her eyes. "Okay, let's do this."

"That's what I'm talkin' about!" Eboni said, smiling. "Now, I'm gonna..."

The chiming of the brass bells hanging from the top of the front door to the school interrupted her.

"You gotta be kiddin' me!" Eboni sighed.

A boy of around twelve or thirteen walked through the doorway, a toothy grin spread across his chubby, chestnut-hued face.

"Welcome to the Afrikan Martial Arts Institute," Remi said, walking toward him. Ebony sauntered behind her.

The boy pressed his palms together beneath his chin in the "prayer" position and then bent deeply at the waist.

"Sank-ah you," he said, affecting a pseudo-Asian accent that sounded like a cross somewhere between Mr. Miyagi and Jackie Chan. "My name is-ah Mark-uh Gah-reen-uh."

"Umm...you *did* hear her say this is the *Afrikan* Martial Arts Institute, didn't you?" Ebony said.

"Yes, ma'am," Mark replied in his normal scratchy voice.

"Then, why in the hell do you sound like you fell out of a damned Sonny Chiba flick?"

"Sonny, who?"

"That's before your time," Remi said. "My name's Remi and this is Eboni. We're instructors here. How can we help you?"

"Actually, I'm here to help *you*," Mark replied, drawing a tape measure out of the pocket of his hooded sweatshirt.

"Is that right?" Remi said.

"Yes, ma'am," Mark said. "When I walked in, I noticed that your school smells a little funky...like a combination of shampoo, sweaty feet and butt crack."

"What?!" Eboni said, taking a step toward Mark. "Little boy..."

"Let him finish," Remi snickered.

"Thank you, ma'am," Mark said. "Now, for a very low price, I can clean the mats and the carpet; keep your school smelling so fresh and so clean-clean."

"How low of a price?" Remi inquired.

"Normally, I'd charge a hundred

dollars every week to come in twice a week and clean the carpet alone," Mark answered. "But, for the price of monthly tuition, I'm willing to clean the carpet *and* the mats, *three* days a week. Now, *that* deal is like a drum with a hole in it...you can't beat it!"

"So, you had this planned before you came in here, didn't you?" Eboni said.

"Of course, Ms. Ahmed." Mark replied. "A school ran by Remi Swan, the former WERK Lightweight Champion...the first – and only – woman to fight men in professional mixed martial arts? And Eboni Ahmed, the undefeated Women's Champion for almost ten years?"

"Not undefeated," Remi said, wagging her index finger. "I *did* defeat her."

"But that wasn't for the title," Mark said, wagging *his* index finger.

"I like this kid," Eboni said.

"So, do we have a deal?" Mark asked.

"We'll give you a shot," Remi replied. "But you'd better not miss a day...of cleaning *or* of training. Do you understand me?"

"Yes, ma'am." Mark answered.

"Come back this evening," Eboni said. "Remi is about to treat me to lunch."

"I am?" Remi said.

"Yeah," Eboni replied. "Since I didn't get to spar, you owe me."

"Well, you heard her," Remi said. "This evening it is. Seven o'clock. Don't be late. You can start cleaning tomorrow."

"Okay, great!" Mark replied as he shuffled toward the door. "Thanks! I'll see you at seven, sharp! Thanks!"

The boy whirled on his heels and dashed out the door.

"Poor kid," Remi said, shaking her head. "He doesn't know what kind of pain he's gotten himself into."

"He gon' learn, today!" Eboni said, doing her best Kevin Hart impression.

She and Remi laughed as they removed the wraps from their fists.

####

Remi pulled the cuffs of her jeans over her biker boots and then slipped on her leather jacket. "You ready?" She called out to Eboni, who was getting dressed in her office.

"Inuh mimnin," a muffled voice came back.

"Huh?" Remi replied.

There was no reply.

Remi leapt from her chair and strode out of her office. "Eboni?"

Eboni staggered out of her office, her palm pressed against the wall as if she was afraid she might collapse. "I said 'in a minute'. Y-you ready?"

"Eboni, what's wrong?" Remi asked, searching Eboni's eyes for the truth.

"Nothing," Eboni replied. "I think I might be coming down with the flu or something. I'm good now, though."

"Maybe I should just take you home."

"Uh-uh," Eboni replied, shaking her head. "You ain't getting' out of buying me lunch *that* easy!"

"Ok," Remi said. "But one more episode and we are getting you checked out."

Remi walked out of the school. Eboni followed her. Remi locked the door and then pulled the gate across it.

"Remi!" Eboni shouted, tapping Remi on the shoulder.

Remi peered over her shoulder. "What's up?"

"Look!" Eboni said, pointing at something across the street.

Remi turned and looked in the direction of Eboni's finger. Mark Green, the twelve year old entrepreneur who had just negotiated his tuition with them, stood with his hands raised above his shoulders. A police officer stood before him, his pudgy, pink fingers clutching a pistol. The muzzle of the pistol was pointed at Mark's forehead.

"Drop the weapon!" The cop demanded.

"Sir, I don't have a weapon," Mark cried. "It's just..."

The cool, autumn air was torn asunder by a thunderous din. Red mist rose from the back of Mark's head and then the boy collapsed.

"Oh, my God!" Remi gasped. "Oh, no!"

"He killed him!" Eboni spat. "He murdered that baby!"

The police officer knelt down beside Mark, his hand slipping inside his police jacket.

Remi sprinted across the street, her heart racing; tears burning her eyes. Eboni ran beside her.

The cop slipped a small, .25 caliber pistol into Mark's palm. He picked up Mark's tape measure, tucked it into his pants pocket and then stood over the boy's body. He looked into Remi's scowling face. "He had a gun," he said with a shrug.

"You goddamned pig!" Eboni shouted, taking a step toward the cop.

The police officer took a step back and aimed his pistol at Eboni's chest. "Get back, or I'll *shoot* your ass!"

Remi's blood pulsed in her ears. Her flesh grew hot. She exploded forward, grabbing the slide of the police officer's pistol.

The cop pulled the trigger, but with the slide held in place within Remi's fist, the gun could not fire.

Remi twisted the barrel of the gun upward and toward the police officer. His trigger finger made a popping noise as it bent at a sickening angle.

The cop screamed in agony. His grip on the pistol weakened.

Remi snatched the gun out of the cop's hand and then slapped him across the temple with the butt of the weapon.

The cop stumbled sideways...right into Eboni's open arms.

Eboni wrapped her arms around his soft waist, clasping her hands behind his lower back. She thrust her hips into his, lifting the rotund police officer off his feet. She then twisted her hips to her right as she raised her arms above her head, launching the cop over her right shoulder.

The cop landed with a loud thud, grunting as his shoulder blades collided with the pavement.

Eboni proceeded to stomp him. Remi hurled the cop's gun into the street and then joined in, driving her heels into the cop's face, belly and groin.

The police officer whimpered, flailing his arms across his face in a weak attempt to protect himself.

Sirens blared in the distance, growing louder with each passing second, but the women continued to stomp and kick...stomp and kick.

Even when other police officers grabbed them, dragging them toward a squad car, they tried to stomp the cop. To trample away what he had done. To make him pay with his life for the young life of Mark Green and all the others who had gone before him by the hand of some murderer in blue and brass.

ROUND TWO

Remi walked down a long, dank hall, escorted by two guards. Her flip-flops beat a soft rhythm upon the concrete floor. A chill slithered over her exposed toes, crept up her legs and then clawed at her spine. The walls of the hall were lined with steel doors. When they arrived at the last set of doors on either side of her, one of the guards opened the door to her right, which was marked 19B in black stencil.

"You've got fifteen minutes, Swan," the guard said.

Remi stepped inside the room. It was small, about the size of a foyer closet. There was a single steel stool in the room that sat before a shatterproof window. On the other side of the window sat Remi's husband, Kundo, who looked up at her with a half-smile.

The door slammed behind her. Remi sat down and leaned forward, bringing her mouth close to the concentric circles of small holes in the center of the window. "Hey baby! How are you? How are Tutu and Ayo?"

"I'm good, love," Kundo replied. "The children are fine; missing mama. I'm missing mama, too."

"I miss y'all," Remi sighed. "Any word?"

"I spoke to Dan," Kundo said. "He's hired *his* lawyer to handle your case. No more public defenders."

"Thank him for me," Remi said. "They're trying to get me to state that Mark pointed a gun at Ferguson and Ferguson had no choice but to shoot him. If I do, I get aggravated battery. If I don't, I get attempted murder."

"Don't say another word to those

bastards!" Kundo spat. "Dan's attorney should be seeing you tomorrow. I'm meeting with a reporter from *Contraband Classified* tomorrow morning and with the Coalition to Combat Police Terrorism tomorrow afternoon; we're gonna blow the lid off this thing, baby! We'll get you and Eboni out of here and get some justice for Mark Green and his family."

"Be careful, Kundo," Remi whispered.

"Always, baby," Kundo replied. "Any word on when they're transferring you upstate?"

"The mayor came by to see me earlier," Remi replied.

"All this press has brought his ass out to try to do some damage control, huh?" Kundo said.

"Yeah," Remi said. "He said the women's prison upstatc is ovcrcrowded and ill equipped to handle the flood of press that will follow Eboni and me there, so they want to keep us closer to home. They are sending us to Ames."

"Ames?"

"It's a new women's facility," Remi answered. "It's an experimental medical facility where imprisoned pregnant women can have their babies and raise them there; or women with psychological issues can receive music therapy and herbal treatment."

"So, Hell dressed up to *look* like Heaven," Kundo said.

"Basically," Remi replied.

The door behind Remi slid open. A guard poked his head in and shouted *"Two minutes!"* The door slammed again.

"Well, baby, I gotta go," Remi sighed as she rose from her seat.

"Stay strong, love," Kundo said. "We'll have you back home soon."

"I know you will, baby."

Kundo kissed his palm and then blew the kiss toward Remi. "I love you."

Remi pretended to catch the kiss in her fist and then pressed it to her chest. "I love you, too."

She turned on her heels and walked out of the room, refusing to allow herself to cry and give the guards something to sell to the press.

Remi sat, cross-legged, in her bunk, listening to Eboni cry her confession. "Are you sure, Eboni?"

"Dementia Pugilistica...Chronic Boxer's Encephalopathy...punch-drunk; whatever you wanna call it, I got it," Eboni replied.

"We're going to get out of here, Eboni," Remi said. "And then, we'll..."

"Mmm...y'all about to make love? Can we watch?"

Remi snapped her head toward the raspy, nasal voice. Standing in the doorway of her cell was an athletically built woman with leathery, alabaster skin and hungry, blue eyes. The woman licked her thin lips, leaving a patch of spittle under her nose. Looming behind the woman in the doorway stood a mountain of thick, bisque flesh that reminded Remi of a great, white whale. *Moby Dick with ratty, blond hair,* she thought.

"I'm P.J.," the woman in the doorway said. "And this here's Katya. She's Russian."

Katya grunted.

Eboni wiped her eyes with her sleeve and then rose from the bed. "Nobody invited you to this party, so beat it!"

A smile crept across P.J.'s face, revealing straight, white teeth. "Oh, I don't need an invitation. This is my pod. Everything – and every*one* – in it belongs to *me.*"

Eboni laughed. "A white girl running things in jail? Since when?"

"Since I was transferred here three months ago from up the road to stand trial for three more niggers they found that I hung in Dacula."

Eboni leapt from the bed and pointed her finger over P.J.'s shoulder.

"Get your ass out of our room before you get hurt, redneck!"

"Look, the only reason I even bothered to pay you this visit is because I know who you two are," P.J. said, taking a step into the room. "I know what you can do with your hands and I respect that. I also know you'll be transferred to Ames in a couple of days."

"So?" Remi replied.

"My girl, here, believes she can beat you in a fight," P.J. said thrusting her finger toward Eboni.

"Please," Eboni grunted.

"You, we're not so sure of," P.J. said to Remi. "That's why you are going to *let* her."

"Take a dive?" Remi inquired.

"It'll do wonders for the Aryan Sisterhood's morale," P.J. answered.

"This chick must have inhaled too much smoke from those burnin' crosses," Eboni said. "Girl, you out yo' rabbit-ass mind!"

"For real," Remi said. "And what are you offering for this favor? A carton of cigarettes? A pack of cookies?

"Your womanhood," P.J. said. "If you don't do this, you'll be giving Katya full body massages...with your tongue...every day until you leave here."

"Now see...now, I'm gonna beat that ass," Eboni said.

Katya took a giant step backward into the common area.

P.J. licked her lips again. "Ain't nothin' between us but space and opportunity out here. My girls already have the guards distracted.

"I got Goliath," Eboni whispered.

"Eboni, let me take her," Remi replied. "You get the redneck."

"Nah, she said that big broad could beat me," Eboni said. "I gotta prove her wrong."

"Okay," Remi said. "Watch out for

shanks."

"Yes, mommy!" Eboni said as she sauntered into the common area.

Remi followed Eboni into the common area – a capacious room, peppered with stainless steel tables with matching benches bolted into the concrete floor – where the inmates ate, played chess, socialized and, occasionally, fought. Tonight, however, it was strangely void of any inmates and quiet as the grave. She perused the room – all the cell doors were closed, but eyes peered out of every tiny window near the top of them. *This was planned*, she thought. She gazed up at the tower – the room that sat above the pod, from where the guards monitored the common area and controlled the doors and lights. It, too, was empty.

P.J. and Katya circled Eboni and Remi like lionesses preparing to pounce on a lone water buffalo. P.J. began rhythmically tapping the side of her head with her fingertips as she took small, shuffling steps toward Remi.

"Fifty-two Blocks?" Remi said as she

bent her knees low, raised her fists to the height of her chin and bent slightly at the waist, assuming a traditional West African martial arts fighting position.

"We call it the Alto Shuffle in here," P.J. replied. "You ain't the only one who knows this jungle-bunny combat stuff."

"Amazing," Remi said.

"What? That a white girl knows the Shuffle?" P.J. snickered.

"No," Remi replied. "That some sister was foolish enough to teach your redneck ass!"

P.J.'s smile twisted into a scowl. "This ain't no ring, jigaboo. Ain't no rules in here. I'm gonna..."

Remi exploded forward, closing on P.J. with blinding speed. She fired a volley of punches into the woman's face. Each powerful blow connected, rending flesh and crushing bone.

P.J.'s arms fell to her sides, her torso stiffened, but her knees became rubbery, wavering from side to side for a brief moment before she collapsed onto her back on the cold, hard floor.

"You talk too much," Remi said, glaring into P.J.'s flitting eyes.

Muffled cheers erupted from inside the cells.

Katya growled and charged toward Eboni with her head down and her massive arms outstretched.

Eboni leapt toward the giant woman, driving her right knee forward with her sinewy hips. Her knee slammed into Katya's chin with a loud crunch.

Katya collapsed onto her haunches.

Eboni darted toward the downed giantess.

Katya thrust her left arm forward, punching Eboni in the gut with her ham-sized fist.

A whoosh of air shot out of Eboni's mouth. She collapsed to her knees, her mouth opening and closing rapidly in an effort to pull air back into her lungs.

Katya shook her head and then struggled to her feet. She held her arms out at her sides to steady herself and then she raised her fists high above her head.

Eboni lurched forward, pressing her torso against Katya's right leg. She wrapped her arms around Katya's thick ankles and then drove her chest forward and downward upon Katya's knee.

Katya screamed as her knee snapped, popped and then bent at an odd angle behind her. She fell onto her side, screaming in agony as she clutched her dislocated knee.

Eboni rose to her feet.

Another cheer came from the cells.

The door to the common area slid open. Eight detention officers rushed into the room.

"On the ground," they barked. "On the ground, now!"

Remi dropped down into a pushup position and then lowered herself until she was prone, with her forehead pressed to the floor. Eboni followed suit.

Remi felt cold hands on her wrists. A moment later, she felt cold steel handcuffs bite into her flesh. She was dragged to her feet by two officers and then shoved out of the common area into the hallway. She was then rushed down the hall and into the laundry room. Remi heard the door slam shut. A moment later, she heard the click of the door being locked.

A woman stepped from behind the dryers. She was dressed in a charcoal-gray, wool business suit with light gray pinstripes. Her straight, black hair was styled in a pageboy haircut and her bistre complexion was flawless. "Hello, Mrs. Swan...Ms. Ahmed," she said. "I am Anna Hess, but you can call me Warden. I run the Ames Medical Facility."

"Did you enjoy the show?" Remi asked.

"Immensely," Warden Hess replied. "The two of you are quite formidable."

"It must have been staged for your

amusement." Remi said.

"I needed to assess your skills," Warden Hess said. "To know you are both the champions I have heard so much about."

"For what?" Eboni hissed. "The only fighting we'll be doing in here is for our lives."

"The men's prisons have seasonal fights," Warden Hess replied. "At these fights, the best fighters from each prison compete in a no-holds barred tournament. The winners of each tournament win the purse for their prison...a purse that is in the tens of millions."

"And?" Remi said.

"And I want you two to represent Ames in the tournament," the Warden replied. "You will be the first women to ever enter."

"Too bad we're inmates, not convicts," Eboni said.

"We all know that will change soon," Warden Hess said. "Look, I will make it worth your while."

"How?" Remi asked.

"I will take three months off your sentence for every fight," Warden Hess answered. "Six months for every win."

"And what, up to three fights per tournament?" Eboni asked.

"Yes," the Warden replied. "Four tournaments a year; so, potentially, you could have two years scratched from your sentence...*if* you win each tournament, of course."

"Fighting men was hard enough in the cage," Remi said. "But these men are fighting for their freedom. They'll fight harder."

"Yeah...and some of them are stone-cold killers or crazy as all get-out," Eboni chimed in.

Warden Hess smiled. "I have a...solution; something that will even the playing field."

"What's that?" Eboni inquired.

"You'll see," the Warden replied. "So, what do you say?"

"We want your guarantee in writing," Remi replied. "But we want *four* months off of our sentences per fight and *nine* months off per win."

"You'd better win big, then," the Warden said. "Okay, it's a deal. Ms. Ahmed, you will fight in the Bantamweight class. Mrs. Swan, you will continue to fight in the Lightweight class. The quarter-final fights are by weight class; the semi-finals are by the drawing of the names from a hat and the winners of the semi finals battle for the championship."

"Wait," Eboni said. "You mean the semi-finals and the finals don't have weight classes? So, I could end up fighting a man who's, literally, twice my size?"

"Or more, yes," Warden Hess replied. "However, like I said, I have something that will even the playing field."

"It better be a machine gun," Eboni sighed.

"What are the weight classes?" Remi

inquired.

"Heavyweight, Middleweight, Lightweight and Bantamweight," Warden Hess answered. "So, I ask again...are you in?"

"Yes," Remi replied.

"Same here," Eboni said.

"Good," Warden Hess said. "The guards will escort you to a van that is waiting to take you to Ames."

"We have to get our stuff," Eboni said.

"Your belongings have already been packed and loaded onto the van," the Warden replied.

"Uh...thanks?" Eboni said.

"Only the best for my fighters," Warden Hess said, smiling. She then turned on her heels and walked away, disappearing in the shadows of the washing machines.

####

Remi and Eboni jogged behind a detention officer – a tall, lean man, whose legs seemed to go on forever – in order to keep pace with his brisk strides. She opened and closed her fists, stretching her liberated wrists, which had been constricted by handcuffs.

"Why did you take the deal?" Eboni whispered. "We should have waited for Dan Wallace's attorney to work his magic."

"I'm buying us time," Remi replied. "Warden Hess would have kept sending her cronies our way until we complied, killed one of those women and got extra time, or got killed ourselves."

"Well, I trust you, so I'm backing your play," Eboni said. "So, don't screw up!"

"I won't," Remi said.

"Stop!" The officer behind them commanded.

Remi and Eboni stopped running and stood, in silence, before a pair of steel double doors marked 'Transport'.

The detention officer at Remi's rear leaned forward until his chin hovered over her shoulder. "Alright ladies, you are about to leave this facility. The men behind this door are armed. If you make any sudden movements, you *will* be put down. If you have to relieve yourselves, hold it; it's just a hop, skip and a jump from here to Ames. If you relieve yourselves on the nice leather interior of that Mercedes van, you will clean it and you will be denied commissary for two months. Do you both understand?"

"Yes," Remi replied.

"I understand, you need a breath mint," Eboni said.

"Funny," the officer said with a smirk.

The doors opened. A black van stood before Remi. Two officers, both dressed in pristine white jumpsuits and white bomber jackets, were posted up beside each open rear door.

The officers were armed with riot shotguns.

Another officer poked his head out of the driver's window. "Hop in, ladies!" He shouted.

Eboni climbed into the van and took a seat. Remi followed her. The officer had not lied – the seats and walls were, indeed made of soft, oxblood leather.

Eboni perused the van and whistled. "Damn, we ridin' in style! This is one of those Mercedes Sprinter Mini-Buses."

"Instead of the whip on our *back*, now we're in the back of the *whip*, huh?" Remi said.

"Yep," Eboni sighed. "We gon' get free, though."

Remi nodded. "Yes, we are."

The ride in the Sprinter was short; no more than fifteen minutes by Remi's estimation. Although the van had windows, they were so thick, so black, she could not see anything when she peered at them except her own reflection. The Sprinter slowed and came to a stop. A moment later, the doors flew open. The guards stood beside them, scatter guns at the ready.

"Out, please," one of the guards said.

Remi stepped out of the van and onto the white, granite floor. Remi looked around. The stone walls, the steel doors, even the light fixtures – all stark white.

Remi and Eboni were led through a door, down a short hallway, to a door marked 'Warden Hess' in ivory text with a black outline.

One of the guards rapped on the door with his knuckles.

A muffled "Come in," came from within the room.

The guard opened the door and stepped inside. The guard at the rear gently nudged Remi and Eboni into the room.

The warden sat at her desk, smiling. "Mrs. Swan, Ms. Ahmed, welcome to Ames Medical Facility. You will be staying in Pod

C. Officers McCray and Dillard here will get you situated. They'll take you on a tour of the facility in the morning."

"Okay," Remi replied.

"I just have a few rules," Warden Hess said. "Most don't apply to you, I'm sure, but I have to tell you anyway. No drugs, except those prescribed by one of our doctors; no fighting other inmates; no martial arts or other combat training outside of the designated training areas, which include the wrestling room, the bag and pad room and the cage; and, finally, since this *is* a medical facility, everyone is kept on a healthy diet tailored for them. All meals will be served in your rooms and eaten there. No meals will be shared with others and every meal must be eaten. Any violation of the rules *will* result in additional time added to your sentence and denial of parole hearings and may result in a stay in solitary confinement, as well. Any questions?"

"No," Remi replied.

"Nope," Eboni said.

"Good," Warden Hess said. "Officer McCray, Officer Dillard…please show the ladies to their rooms."

"Yes, ma'am," Officer McCray said.

"On it, Warden," Officer Dillard replied.

"Follow me, ladies," Officer Dillard said, peering over his shoulder.

He marched out of the room. Eboni followed. Remi walked behind her. Officer Dillard led them to the end of the hall to an elevator door. The door slid open and everyone stepped inside the elevator. Remi noticed that the elevator only had a button for the first and second floor.

"This prison only has two floors?" Remi said.

"This isn't a prison," Officer McCray said. "It's a medical facility. And why do you ask? Planning an escape attempt?"

"If it's just a medical facility, we're free to leave whenever we want, right?" Remi said.

"You're free to leave when the Warden says you're well enough to," Officer McCray said. "And before you ask, yes, she's a doctor."

The door slid open. Remi followed Officer Dillard down a hallway. On her left were the pods – capacious rooms that housed several cells and a central common area. On her left were the towers for each pod – where the officers sat, keeping watch over the activities within the pod, controlling the pod and cell doors and relaxing until they had to transport an inmate or respond to some crisis. Remi counted four pods. Her pod, 'C', was next to last. She assumed the last pod was 'D'.

"Open Pod C," Officer Dillard shouted.

"Opening Pod C!" Someone shouted from the tower.

The pod's door slid open.

"You're home, ladies," Officer McCray said. "You're in room four. You will find your uniforms, towels and toiletries there. Shower and change. Leave those old blue uniforms at your door. You have twenty minutes, then your door will lock and your light will go out. The other ladies are already locked down for the night."

Remi and Eboni sauntered toward their cell – the only one with an open door. Women whistled and catcalled.

"You pretty!"

"Wanna be my girlfriend?"

"Hey, sis, bless me with those blues when you change out into your whites, okay?"

Remi ignored the voices and kept her gaze on her door. She stepped into her room. It was as stark white and clean as everything else she had seen in this facility, thus far.

"Damn, is the training equipment white, too?" Eboni said, shaking her head.

"If it is, it won't be after we get a hold of it," Remi replied.

"I know that's right," Eboni said,

extending her fist.

Remi pressed her fist to Eboni's and then extended her fingers as she retracted her hand. Eboni mirrored her, simulating an explosion.

"Age before beauty," Remi said, nodding toward the shower in their bathroom.

"I'm older *and* more beautiful, so I guess I'll have to take *two* showers," Eboni replied.

"You should write a book, too," Remi said. "Your imagination is tremendous!"

"Whatever," Eboni replied with a smirk. "So, how are we gonna let Kundo know we're here?"

"I told him the transfer was coming," Remi said. "Dan Wallace's attorney is coming to see us tomorrow. When they tell him we've been transferred, he'll know to come here."

"Cool," Eboni replied. "We gotta get out of here ASAP, Remi...that warden gives me the creeps."

"Me too," Remi said. "Until we get out of here, we move as a unit, we sleep with one eye open, we don't start nothin', but we sure as hell finish it."

Eboni pounded her left palm with her right fist. "Damn skippy!"

ROUND THREE

"It is seven a.m., time to wake up," a soothing, maternal voice crooned from what sounded to Remi like several speakers – all obviously concealed within the walls and ceiling because the only fixtures in her cell were the lights and a small plasma television embedded in the wall above the white oak desk opposite the bunks. *"It is seven a.m., time to wake up,"* the voice said again.

"Shut *up!*" Eboni hissed, throwing her pillow at the wall.

Remi sat upright, dangling her feet over the edge of the bed. "I guess it's time for breakfast. We'd better get up."

"*You'd* better get your feet out of my face," Eboni said.

"You're just jealous of my pretty feet," Remi replied.

"You do keep 'em lookin' nice," Eboni said, sitting up. "Kundo must have a thing for toes."

"I ain't sayin' nothin'," Remi snickered.

Eboni laughed. "Yep, that's my answer, right there."

A click came from the door. A moment later, it slid open. A short, athletically built woman dressed in a white officer's uniform pushed a chrome cart into the room. Atop the cart were two white, polymer trays. Remi peered down at the multi-compartmented trays – both of them contained steaming oatmeal, a banana, a bunch of grapes and a toasted cinnamon raison bagel. Beside each tray was a tall plastic cup full of what looked like a green smoothie.

"Good morning, ladies," the officer said. "I'm Officer Reed. I'm here to work with you during the day shift. Eat up...all of it and enjoy."

"Where's the steak and eggs?" Eboni asked, staring at the tray in despair. "The salmon croquettes? The pancakes? The turkey bacon?"

"All of our patients are placed on a strict diet designed to promote health, fitness and focus," Officer Reed replied. "All meals are vegetarian and vegan."

"Aw, hell naw!" Eboni protested.

Remi snickered. "Welcome to my world."

The women removed their trays and cups from the cart and placed them on the table.

"I'll return for the trays and cups in an hour," Officer Reed said. "Throw away the plasticware. If there are any stains on your clothing, yell up to the pod and let us know; an officer will bring you a fresh pair. The Warden doesn't permit anyone to leave their pod with any stains on their whites. I'll return at nine to take you on a tour of the facility."

Officer Reed pushed the cart out of the room. The door closed behind her.

"Patients?" Eboni whispered.

"I know, right?" Remi replied.

"I guess they think it sounds better than inmate or convict," Eboni said.

"Or, we're all part of some damned experiment," Remi said. "Why is it a rule that we eat all of our food?"

"Shoot, girl," Eboni said, scooping a mound of oatmeal into her mouth with her spoon. "Damn, this is good. Eating all our food ain't the problem. This small ass portions are!"

"Greedy," Remi said, shaking her head. "Well...bon appetite."

"Yeah, we gon' be bony and petite eatin' like this," Eboni replied.

Remi giggled and then gobbled down a spoonful of the sweet oatmeal. "This *is* good," she said. "I haven't had oatmeal this good since Kundo made me that breakfast for Mother's Day four years ago.

The rest of the meal was terrible, but that oatmeal was delicious! I...

The words died in her throat. An overwhelming feeling of loneliness fell over her like a blanket – a quilt made of patches of despair that threatened to smother her. Tears burst from the corners of her eyes; her shoulders shook as she cried.

Eboni placed a gentle hand on her shoulder. "I know you miss him, girl. Your babies, too. One way or another, you gon' see them again, soon. We gon' get out of here."

"Or die trying," Remi said.

"Either way, we're out," Eboni replied. "Now, stop cryin' so I can stop comfortin', 'cause if my oatmeal gets cold, we gon' have a problem up in here!"

Remi laughed. She picked up her spoon and went back to eating her breakfast.

####

The cell door slid open. Officer Reed

entered the room, pushing her cart before her.

"Did you enjoy your meal, ladies?" She asked. Ready to go?

"Yes and yes," Remi replied.

"Good," Officer Reed said, stacking one tray on top of the other on the cart. "I'll be back after I collect all of the trays."

Officer Reed exited the room.

A half hour later, she returned. "Come on ladies," she said.

Remi and Eboni walked out of the cell behind Officer Reed. Nearly a dozen women sat in the common area, playing cards, chess and various board games.

"Listen up, ladies!" Officer Reed commanded.

Everyone looked up from their games and focused their attention on Officer Reed.

"These are your new pod mates," Officer Reed began. "Remi Swan and Eboni Ahmed. You have probably heard of them. Give them their space...and their respect. Understood?"

The women expressed their understanding with grunts, groans, "yeses" and "yeps."

"Good," Officer Reed said. "I'll make sure you all get a week shaved off your sentence, for being so agreeable"

Eboni nudged Remi with her elbow. "Time is currency in here," she whispered.

"Each pod houses ten to sixteen patients, with up to two patients per room," Officer Reed said, peering over her shoulder. "Follow me."

Officer Reed sauntered to the pod door. She raised her hand high above her head, signaling the tower to open the door. The door slid open and Officer Reed, Eboni and Remi stepped out of the pod into the main hallway.

"There are the four pods, the administrative offices and an infirmary on this floor," Officer Reed said. "You've seen the administrative offices and you know where Warden Hess' office is; let's check out the infirmary."

Remi and Eboni followed Officer Reed past Pod D to the end of the hall. She stood before what appeared to be an unmarked, white wall. She placed her palms against the smooth stone. A humming din rose from the floor. Officer Reed removed her hands from the wall. A second later, the wall slid downward, disappearing into the floor.

Eboni whistled. "Damn!"

Before them, men and women dressed in white frocks over their white medical uniforms, hustled and bustled about, caring for a few patients who lay on chrome beds that were positioned against each wall and moving in and out of rooms that appeared to be made of very thick glass.

"We have three doctors and nine nurses on staff," Officer Reed said. "We also have a lab tech and a pharmacist."

"And then, there's me," a voice came from their left.

Remi looked toward the voice. A

woman, who appeared to be in her mid-forties, sat in a wheelchair. The chair was made of chrome and white leather. The woman's long, straight hair was nearly as white as the leather and her skin was just a shade darker.

"I'm Peggy," the woman said, smiling.

"And what do you do here, Peggy?" Remi asked.

Peggy's smile faded. Her eyes locked onto Remi's. A chill slithered up Remi's spine.

"Um...Peggy is our psychotherapist," Officer Reed said. "And..."

"And that chill you felt proves that attention regulates emotion," Peggy said, interrupting Officer Reed. "My change in facial expression and mood caused you to focus on the sudden and odd change, which caused a change in your emotions. I know you all felt it."

"O...kay," Remi replied.

"That's what I do here," Peggy

replied. "I work to discover the best methods for quieting an agitated and unruly amygdala – the two almond-shaped groups of nuclei located within the temporal lobes of the brain that perform a primary role in the processing of memory, decision-making, and emotional reactions. I..."

A loud bestial noise, like the sound of an angry duet sung by a raging gorilla and a cornered cat, erupted from one of the glass rooms.

"Janine is unhappy," Peggy said. "Follow me. I'll show you, first hand, how my methods work."

"Brace yourselves," Officer Reed whispered.

"For what?" Remi replied, walking behind Peggy, whose motorized wheelchair cruised toward a room on the far wall.

"For that," Officer Reed said, pointing toward the room.

Behind the glass wall stood what appeared to be a giant, hairless chimpanzee. The creature's skin was brownish-red, as was the unkempt afro that sat upon its large, square-shaped head. Janine – as Peggy had called the creature – stood nearly seven feet tall, her well-defined forearms were the size of a muscular man's calf and her upper arms were nearly as big as a man's thigh. Small breasts under her white t-shirt shook as Janine roared again. Janine's open mouth revealed a set of large, perfectly white teeth with elongated canine teeth.

Remi recognized, underneath Janine's bestial face, eyes that were quite human and in emotional pain.

"Oh, my God," Remi said. "That...that's a woman!"

"A child, actually," Officer Reed said. "Janine is thirteen. She was born here."

"Born here?" Remi replied, shaking her head. "How? This is a new facility."

"Not new," Officer Reed said. "Just new to the public."

"I want out of here, now!" Eboni said. "What did y'all do to her? This place is some sort of laboratory...and we're the rats!"

"Calm down!" Officer Reed ordered, pulling a white baton from her waist. "Or I'll be forced to put you down."

"With that little toothpick?" Ebony said. "Let's see."

Officer Reed's fist tightened around the handle of the baton. White sparks flashed from the shaft of the weapon. The baton crackled and hummed. "You'd be...shocked at what this 'little toothpick' can do." She said.

"Shocked...funny," Eboni said. "I'll play nice, for now, Reed."

"Thank you," Officer Reed replied. "One of our original patients gave birth to Janine before dying from some undeterminable illness. We have been raising her here ever since."

Peggy rolled up to the window before Janine. She pressed a button on the armrest of her wheelchair. "Janine? Janine, can you hear me?"

Janine slowly looked toward the

window. She slammed her massive hands into the glass, causing the room to shake. Remi jumped. Janine roared again, pounding her chests with her fists.

"Can she get out of there?" Remi asked.

"No," Officer Reed answered. "Luckily, that glass is damn near indestructible. If Janine gets out and is agitated, we'd have a problem."

"I bet," Eboni said.

Peggy reached into her frock pocket and retrieved a piece of paper. She stared at the paper for a few moments and then burst into tears.

Janine stopped roaring and beating her chest. She stared at Peggy and craned her neck in an attempt to see what was on the paper.

Peggy reached into her frock pocket again. This time, she retrieved a large, very colorful lollipop. "I bought this for my granddaughter," she said, smiling at Janine. "But she was bad yesterday. She threw a tantrum and raised her voice at her mother, so I'm giving it to you...*if* you want it."

Janine smiled and nodded her head.

Peggy rolled to Janine's door. She opened the hatch at the bottom of it and slid the lollipop inside. Janine ambled to the door, picked up the lollipop with her sausage-sized fingers and sat, cross-legged on the floor, sucking the sweet confection.

Peggy turned to face Remi and Eboni. "And that is how you calm the amygdala."

"Why are you showing us all of this?" Remi asked. "Isn't this top secret stuff here?"

"Who are you going to tell?" Peggy said, smiling.

"My attorney is coming to see me, today," Remi said. "I could tell him."

Peggy shot a glance at Officer Reed. "They don't know?"

"I haven't had a chance to tell

them," Officer Reed replied.

"Tell us what?" Remi inquired.

"The attorney Dan Wallace hired to represent you and your husband were in a terrible car accident last night."

Remi's knees felt as if they had turned to jelly. Her jaws tightened until they hurt and her heart felt as if it would leap from her chest. "Why in the hell didn't your ass tell me?"

"My orders were to say nothing until we were in the infirmary," Officer Reed replied. "Kundo is okay. He is in stable condition at Emory. The attorney, however, didn't make it."

"God damn," Eboni sighed.

"Take me back to my room," Remi said.

"My orders..."

"Damn your orders!" Remi said, taking a step toward Officer Reed. "Take me back to my room!"

A stabbing pain assaulted Remi's

right thigh. She looked down at her leg. Peggy withdrew a needle from it.

"Gotcha," Peggy said, smiling. "Got your friend, too."

Remi snapped her head toward Eboni. Eboni staggered sideways, her arms outstretched in an attempt to balance herself. Remi's vision blurred. The world began to spin and tilt. All the white around her turned to blackness. A blackness accompanied by a silence quieter than the grave.

####

Remi opened her eyes. High above her was a white ceiling with several rows of white track lights. She sat bolt upright and then perused her surroundings. Eboni stirred on a cot beside her. Several brown leather heavy bags hung, at various lengths, from the ceiling. The floor was covered by scores of white mats that fit together like a jigsaw puzzle. Beside her mat was a tray. Upon the tray were moderate portions of squash, broccoli, baked beans and rice. Next to the tray was a purple-hued smoothie.

"Eat up. Your training begins in fifteen minutes."

Remi peered over her shoulder. Warden Hess stood behind her, smiling.

"My husband..." Remi began.

"Is fine," Warden Hess replied, cutting her off. "The doctors say he suffered some bruising and a minor concussion, but he will be discharged in a day or two."

Eboni sat up. "When can we speak to him?"

"Eat up," the warden said. "Finish your lunch and your dinner and I promise, I will arrange for you both to talk to him tomorrow morning."

"What's up with the food?" Remi said. "Why is it so important to everyone that we eat every drop?"

"We have spent a lot of money studying diet's effect on mood and on athletic performance," Warden Hess replied. "If we can improve your strength and your endurance, while keeping your mood balanced..."

"You'll make a ton of money by cornering the market on performance enhancing drugs," Eboni said.

"Bingo," Warden Hess replied.

"So, you're subjecting us to steroids in our food?" Remi said.

"No," Warden Hess said. "Not steroids. Something much more potent; more...thorough. Take you, for instance, Miss Ahmed."

Eboni raised an eyebrow. "What about me?"

"You were suffering the effects of chronic boxer's encephalopathy, were you not?" Warden Hess said.

Eboni shot a glance at Remi. Remi shrugged.

"You monitored our conversations back at the Rice Street facility," Eboni said.

"Of course," Warden Hess replied. "I told you, I studied you both thoroughly before bringing you here. Back to the subject at hand, though. Ms. Ahmed, you haven't slurred your speech since you have been here; you haven't lost your balance – except, of course, when Peggy injected you in the infirmary and that had nothing to do with your condition."

"So, you'd have us believe that after one meal, I'm miraculously healed?" Eboni said.

"No, not healed," Warden Hess replied. "In another week, however, the improvements will be permanent and no matter how many blows to the head you suffer, encephalopathy will not be an issue."

"So, you've altered our DNA, like that poor girl Janine back in the infirmary?" Remi said.

"Janine was born with her genetic defect," Warden Hess said. "Her mother came to us with stage-four pancreatic cancer. Our program eradicated the cancer, but had unfortunate effects on the baby growing in her womb."

Remi stood up, staring into Warden Hess' eyes. "If I find out you have done something harmful to us, I'm going to kill you."

"Fair enough," Warden Hess said. "Now, please, eat; you have ten minutes before your training begins."

Warden Hess smiled, turned away from Remi and then sauntered out of the training room.

"These bastards murdered that lawyer and hurt Kundo," Eboni whispered.

"Yep," Remi replied. "They want us to fight in their tournaments; to prove that whatever in the hell they are feeding us works."

"So, we start killin'?" Eboni said.

"Not yet," Remi replied.

"What then?" Eboni asked.

"We eat; we play along for now," Remi answered, grabbing her fork and waving it about. "Traveling to and from that tournament might provide us with an opportunity to escape."

"Okay," Eboni said, raising her cup of smoothie. "To Kundo!"

Remi picked up her cup and tapped Eboni's cup with it. "To Kundo!"

####

Officers Dillard and McCray walked into the training room. They were both dressed in sweat-suits – white, of course.

"On your feet, ladies," Officer Dillard shouted. "Time to work on those strikes."

"Aw snap!" Eboni said, sliding her try under her cot. "Are we sparring? I hope you ate your Wheaties today, Officer Dillard."

"No sparring," Officer Dillard said. "That is reserved for the cage, which is in the room next door. But you don't want none, anyway, Ms. Ahmed."

"Oh, I do," Eboni said. "Knocking out five-o would get me some cred in here."

"Isn't that what got you here in the

first place?" Officer Dillard said.

"What *got me here* was me exactin' justice for the murder of one of our babies," Eboni replied.

"Well, exact some justice on these bags," Officer McCray said. "Ten three-minute rounds; with a one minute rest between rounds. Wraps and gloves are in the panels on the wall to your left."

Eboni pointed at the heavy bag nearest to her. "I'm gonna name this bag Dillard." She pointed to another bag to her left. "And I'll call this one McCray."

"Whatever works," Officer Dillard said with a shrug.

Eboni shuffled toward the bag and then unleashed a quick punch and kick combination upon it. Each strike on the bag sounded like a crack of lightning.

A bead of sweat rolled down Officer Dillard's forehead. He swallowed hard.

Remi whirled on the ball of her left foot as she raised her right knee to her belly. She thrust her foot behind her, driving her heel into the heavy bag at her rear. The bag collapsed around Remi's foot. Remi brought her foot down with a jerk and then turned to face the bag, striking it with a powerful right cross. The bag nearly bent in half.

McCray shot a glance at Dillard. "Damn," he whispered.

Remi paused. She was strong, but she never felt so powerful, so alive. A powerful impulse to attack the heavy bag overcame her. Her heart raced and an urge to fight; to destroy rose, like an inferno, in her gut. She tried to calm herself, to no avail. A growl rose in her throat. She leapt forward, slamming the side of her forehead into the bag. She then wrapped her left arm around the bag and drove a volley of elbow strikes into it.

"Time!"

Remi stepped away from the bag. The leather covering of the bag had split in several spots. Bits of cloth burst from the tears. "That couldn't have been three minutes," she said.

"It was," McCray replied.

To Remi, it felt like only seconds had passed. She glanced at Eboni, who looked just as confused as she was. Eboni's bag was deeply dented in the middle, giving it the appearance of an old soda bottle.

"Round two!" Dillard shouted.

Remi smiled. She couldn't wait to pound the bag again. She couldn't wait.

####

"I godda feewin'...

I got a feewin' sisdas..

I godda feewin'...

Someblonny's twine do bweak dis link,

Budda hope godda lipeboat whis hiship sink."

Remi was awakened by a mumbled, off-beat rendition of her signature ring entry chant.

She sat up and looked down in the direction of the voice. Eboni sat at the desk, rocking back and forth. Her eyes were slightly crossed and a crooked smile was spread across her face. A line of spittle trickled from the corner of her mouth.

Remi leapt out of the bed and knelt before her friend. "Eboni?"

Eboni gazed at Remi with dull eyes and smiled. "Huh?"

"Oh, my god!" Remi gasped. "Help! Somebody help!"

The cell door slid open. Officer Reed rushed in. "What's the problem?"

"It's Eboni," Remi replied. "She...something's wrong with her...she's not...right."

"Officer Reed pulled a radio from her belt. "We have a possible Code Ninety-nine in C-4. We have a possible Code Ninety-nine in C-4."

"Copy that," a voice squawked from the radio. *"En route."*

"Ms. Ahmed, help is coming soon,"

Officer Reed said.

"Why?" Eboni replied. "I fee-o fibe."

"They just want to check you out before your fight," Remi lied. She took a deep breath and clenched her fists to help her fight back the tears that threatened to burst forth. "Routine stuff."

"Wokay," Eboni replied.

After what seemed to Remi like forever, two of the infirmary's medics trotted into the cell with a gurney. They lowered the stretcher to the height of Eboni's knees.

"Hop on," Remi said. "They're giving you a free ride."

Eboni smiled broadly at Remi. "Wokay."

The medics raised the gurney and wheeled Eboni out. Officer Reed followed them. She paused, peering over her shoulder at Remi.

"We're going to take good care of her," she said. "I'll let you know Ms.

Ahmed's condition as soon as I know something."

"Thank you," Remi replied.

The cell door slid shut. Remi walked over to the bunk and plopped down onto Eboni's bed. She sat, slumped, in silence as a torrent of tears stained her face.

The cell door slid open. Remi hopped to her feet.

Warden Hess sauntered into the room carrying Remi's lunch tray and smoothie. "Mrs. Swan, how are you?"

"I've been better," Remi replied. "How's Eboni? Officer Reed said she was going to let me know something, but it's been hours."

Warden Hess sat the tray and cup on Remi's desk. "I wanted to deliver the news to you myself and to escort you to infirmary for your massage before we head down to Baldwin for the tournament."

"So...?" Remi replied.

"Ms. Ahmed has suffered a transient ischemic attack - a temporary episode of brain dysfunction caused by the loss of blood flow to the brain," Warden Hess replied.

"I know what a TIA is," Remi said. "So, her punch drunkenness became more aggressive?"

"Yes."

"How?"

Warden Hess took a step toward Remi. Her expression was like granite. "Sit down, Mrs. Swan. I am going to explain something to you."

"I'd rather stand," Remi said.

"Sit down," Warden Hess said. "You want answers? Sit!"

Remi sat on the lower bunk. Warden Hess sat in the chair opposite her.

"Ms. Ahmed's TIA was caused by an adverse reaction to a virus that was in her food," the warden said.

"A virus?" Remi said. "How did it get

in the food? Why aren't I sick? Are any other women ill?"

"We put it in the food," Warden Hess replied.

"You what?" Remi bellowed.

"Calm yourself," Warden Hess said. "There are officers outside this door. If they come in, you'll be taken to the tournament without the answers you seek. That confusion could adversely affect your performance. We don't want that."

"You think I'm fighting in a damned tournament for you now?" Remi said, shaking her head. "*Hell* no!"

"If you don't, I will be forced to deny your friend the antivirus that she so desperately needs," Warden Hess replied. "And don't forget, your husband is home, now, but he is still recovering. It would be terrible if he suffered some set back...but these things *do* happen."

"You set this up," Remi said.

"No, we did not," Warden Hess replied. "We call our little creation

AMVO...a-m-v-o – Adrenal Myostatin Viral Organism. AMVO halts the production of myostatin – a protein that inhibits the growth of muscles, preventing them from growing too large. At the same time, it increases the production of adrenaline."

"So, it makes its victims bigger, stronger and more aggressive," Remi said.

"In theory," Warden Hess said. "But viruses often mutate with unexpected results. AMVO works differently in each patient. Take Janine for instance...her mother was one of our earlier patients. She, like all of the early patients, fell ill and died. Janine, who was born with the virus, however, grew to incredible proportions and is possessed of strength far beyond any normal man. It is her blood that we now harvest the virus from."

"So, this AMVO is contagious?" Remi inquired.

"Janine is the only patient who has manifested AMVO as a contagion and even then, the virus must be either ingested or injected," Warden Hess replied.

"But Eboni's punch drunkenness seemed to be healed," Remi said.

"It did heal," Warden Hess said. "But in healing one part of Ms. Ahmed's brain, it left another part weakened...and it is trying to spread. We have halted its spread and have the antivirus prepared. Once you win that tournament, I will call them and they will give her the antivirus. She has about ten hours before the virus grows immune to the meds we are using to halt its spread, so we have plenty time."

"What if I lose?" Remi said.

"You won't," Warden Hess said, rising from the chair. "Ms. Ahmed and your husband are counting on you."

Warden Hess stepped to the door. The door slid open and the warden stepped out. Officers Dillard and McCray stood just beyond the doorway.

"Eat up," Warden Hess said as she walked away.

Remi stared at her tray and the cup. A wave of nausea rose in her gut. She sat down, fighting the urge to vomit and ate her virus-laden lunch.

ROUND FOUR

The roar of the crowd was deafening. Remi perused the arena. The domed, elliptical-shaped room appeared to be carved from a single piece of crimson granite. The spectators sat in plush, navy blue, leather chairs. She, along with the other fighters, sat on a long stone bench that was situated a few feet from one side of the octagonal cage, which sat high above the arena floor.

Three guards stood at both ends of the bench. Their heads were covered with shiny blue helmets and their faces hid behind blue-tinted, plastic face shields. Their navy blue jumpsuits peeked from underneath padded gauntlets, elbow pads, shoulder pads, knee pads and greaves. Each man held a stun baton at the ready. A pair of guards escorted each prisoner to opposite sides of the ring when it was their time to fight.

The Bantamweight quarter finals were done. And the first Lightweight fight was over. The fights were brutal, with only four rules: no biting; no attacks to the eyes; no attacks to the groin and no weapons. The fights had no time limit, only ending when one fighter submitted, was knocked unconscious or was killed.

The spectators – corporate types and other men and women with wealth, by the looks of them – loved the bloody spectacle. Remi recognized a few politicians, religious leaders, professional athletes and celebrity entertainers among the salivating crowd.

"Hold on to your seats folks!" The announcer – a lanky, middle-aged man who was introduced as Jason Liu, veteran star of Chinese martial arts cinema – bellowed. "We have an undefeated, undisputed champion in our midst...and the first female fighter to shed blood in this cage!"

"The crowd howled, stomped and whistled.

Hailing from Atlanta, Georgia," Jason Liu shouted. "She really needs no introduction...from Ames Medical Facility; she is an indigenous African martial arts fighter weighing in at one hundred fifty-five pounds...Remi 'The Single Link' Swan!"

The crowd cheered.

Remi leapt to her feet. She jogged to the cage, with a guard at each flank. The closer she got to the octagon, the stronger she felt. Her very bones seethed with energy. She pushed the cage door open and sprinted inside, shuffling sideways around Jason Liu.

The crowd roared.

Remi ran to her corner. She raised her fists to her chin as she shuffled in place from side-to-side.

"And now," Jason began. "Hailing from Coastal State prison, via Brooklyn, New York...he is a Fifty-Two Blocks fighter...weighing in at one-hundred fifty-seven pounds...Wallace 'Mr. Fifty-Two' Himes!"

The crowd cheered.

"Are you ready?" Jason Liu asked, pointing at Remi.

She nodded. The urge to destroy her opponent raged in her gut.

"Are you ready?" Jason asked Mr. Fifty-Two.

"Hell yeah!" Mr. Fifty-Two shouted.

"Fight!" Jason commanded.

Remi shuffled forward.

Mr. Fifty-Two darted forward, rhythmically tapping his elbows with the tips of his fingers. He exploded toward Remi, launching a lightning fast flurry of hooks and uppercuts toward Remi's chin.

Remi raised her elbows, moving them like pistons, the dense muscles of her forearms and biceps absorbing the force of Mr. Fifty-Two's hook punches. She then drove her right elbow downward, slamming the bony tip of it into the small bones of Mr. Fifty-Two's uppercutting fist.

Mr. Fifty-Two wailed in agony. He staggered backward, shaking his shattered left hand, as if he was trying to cast off the pain.

Remi leapt forward, thrusting her knee toward Mr. Fifty-Two's chest. The powerful flying knee slammed into Mr. Fifty-Two's sternum.

A loud crack erupted from Mr. Fifty-Two's chest. He gasped as his shoulders folded inward, nearly touching each other. He collapsed onto his face.

Remi stood over Mr. Fifty-Two, staring, in horror, at the damage she had done. Her power, her speed and her ferocity frightened her. She had wanted to kill Mr. Fifty-Two and perhaps she had.

Four medics rushed into the cage with a stretcher. They rolled Mr. Fifty-Two onto it and then jogged out of the octagon.

Jason grabbed Remi's wrist and raised her hand above her head. "The winner, by knockout...Remi 'The Single Link' Swan!"

The spectators went wild.

"The Single Link moves on to the Semi-Finals!" Jason said.

The cage door opened. Remi sauntered out of the cage, where two guards met her. She was escorted back to her seat on the bench. She felt the eyes of the other fighters locked on her, but she didn't return their gaze.

I'm going to kill Warden Hess for what she's done to me, she thought. *For what she's done to Eboni.*

####

The fights raged for hours. Remi had run through her opponents, defeating them with ease, as if she was fighting toddlers. Now, she stood opposite the reigning Lightweight champion in the cage. 'Pisces' Pete Tottenham was the only fighter who had ever successfully used internal Chinese martial arts in the ring. Pisces' mastery of the circular, evasive Bagua Zhang and the explosive, linear Xing Yi Quan and his experience in using them on the streets of Chicago and in prisons across America made him an unpredictable and dangerous fighter.

Pisces bent his knees a bit and extended his palms toward Remi.

Remi brought her right foot forward, bent her knees and raised her left heel as she brought up her fists to the height of her chin in her customary, boxing-like African fighting position. The urge to destroy Pisces rose in Remi's chest. She fought to kill the urge; to center herself. *This is just a sporting match,* she told herself. But the urge to kill; to utterly eradicate Pisces would not be quieted.

Pisces smirked. In Remi's mind, he was telling her, without words that she was unworthy. That he would defeat her because her skills were of no comparison to his. That the indigenous African martial arts were like child's-play when measured against the superior Asian ones.

Remi roared and charged forward.

Pisces coiled his back and then skittered forward.

Remi thrust her left forward, driving

her heel toward Pisces' liver.

Pisces rolled his shoulders and hips to his right. Remi's kick shot past him. Pisces took advantage of the miss, driving his hips back toward his center as he struck with his open right palm. His palm plowed into Remi's solar plexus.

Remi staggered backward from the blow. The air rushed from her lungs.

Pisces closed on Remi with surprising speed.

Remi needed a few moments to catch her breath; moments Pisces seemed reluctant to give her. She threw a jab in desperation.

Pisces' left arm deflected Remi's punch past his shoulder as he reached for her throat with the thumb, index and middle fingers of his right hand. Pisces' thumb and fingers dug into Remi's throat. He squeezed.

Remi's throat threatened to collapse under the power of Pisces' claw-like grip. She tensed the muscles in her neck to give her a bit of relief. She stepped far back with her right leg, raised her left elbow just above the height of Pisces' forearm and then shifted to her right, driving her elbow into his arm. The combined force of her turning body and her elbow, forced Pisces to release his crushing grasp.

Pisces launched a looping, diagonal hook punch toward Remi's temple.

Remi raised her elbow to the height of her brow, absorbing the blow with her arm. She then shuffled forward and then struck with a rear knee that slammed into the inside of Pisces' right thigh like a wrecking ball.

Pisces' thigh bent outward with a loud crack. He screamed as his leg gave out, collapsing sideways.

Remi dropped to her right knee. She wrapped her arms around Pisces' left thigh and then drove her chest into it, slamming Pisces onto his back. She shoved Pisces' foot into her armpit and drove the blade of her wrist into his Achilles tendon as she arched backward.

Pisces wailed as the tendons of his

foot were torn from the muscles of his calf and his foot.

Remi tossed Pisces' now lifeless foot to the side and then slid up his body, straddling his waist. Remi raised both fists high above her head.

"Please, don't," Pisces begged.

Remi drove her fists downward, slamming them into both sides of Pisces' collar bone.

A shriek escaped Pisces' lips as his collarbone pulverized under the crushing power of Remi's hammer-fists. His eyes rolled about in their sockets and then his body fell limp.

Remi raised her fists again. Her fists shook and her heart pounded with the anticipation of flattening Pisces' skull.

"Kill him! Kill him!" The crowd chanted.

Remi's killing impulse raged. *Always give them what they want,* she thought. Remi's muscles tensed. She expanded her chest and raised her fists higher. *Wait...no, I...I can't. I shouldn't...*

"Kill him! Kill him!"

I'm going to pound his skull like yam!

"Kill him! Kill him!"

A ki i tori-i gbigbo pa aja – you don't kill a dog for barking.

The heat in Remi's chest cooled. The raging tempest in her mind dissipated, leaving in its wake a light breeze. She leapt to her feet and backed away from Pisces' unconscious body.

Jason Liu grabbed Remi's wrist and raised her fist in the air. "The winner...and new champion of the Lightweight Division is Remi 'The Single Link' Swan!"

The crowd cheered.

Remi walked to the door of the cage, a guard opened it. She was led by the guards back to her seat.

"Remi will go on to fight Stanley 'The Beast' Frank, the undefeated Heavyweight and tournament Champion for the past five years," Jason Liu said. "We will have an hour intermission before the Grand Championship, so eat, drink and be merry before The Single Link and The Beast go to war!"

The spectators, whistled, clapped and stomped in approval.

"Let's go, Swan," A guard commanded.

Remi rose from the bench and followed the guard to a door behind her. A pair of guards walked behind her. The guard at the front opened the door. Remi entered and the guards followed her inside. Warden Hess stood before her.

"Excellent job!" Warden Hess said with a smile.

"You have turned me into a goddamned monster!" Remi spat.

"A very *powerful* monster, though," Warden Hess replied. "Now, please, sit," she said, pointing toward a massage chair.

Remi sat in the chair and placed her chest upon the support. Warden Hess massaged Remi's shoulders firmly, but gently.

"I was once the leading Orthopedic and Neurological Physical Therapist in the United States," the warden said. "I miss the work."

"You should return to it," Remi said. "Before Ames becomes the death of you."

Warden Hess continued with her massage. "Is that a threat?"

"A warning," Remi said. "I now understand why you keep Eboni and me segregated from the other prisoners, though...can't have a bunch of physically enhanced monsters starting a riot."

"None of the other women – other than Ms. Ahmed and Janine - possess your...attributes," Warden Hess replied. "In fact, most of them are dying. We don't know exactly how this virus works. One of the dying women might have caused you to get sick, too."

Warden Hess placed a palm on Remi's chin and one on the crest of her head. She then pushed with small movements in one direction while she pulled in the other, pulling Remi's neck and upper spine into alignment. "When I'm done, I want you to soak for fifteen minutes in the Epsom salt and arnica leaf bath we have prepared for you in the Jacuzzi just beyond those curtains," she said, pointing toward the left corner of the room, which had a thick, brown curtain stretched across it. "Then I want you to stretch and do a light warm up until you're called."

"Ok," Remi replied.

"Tell me something," Warden Hess began.

"Yes?"

"When you had Pisces on the ground, why didn't you kill him?"

"Because I'm not a murderer."

"No, I mean, I know you felt the impulse to do it; it was all over your face," Warden Hess said. "How did you keep control?"

"My training," Remi said. "A Yoruba Proverb brought me back to sanity.

Whenever I feel lost, the words of my answers always provide a guiding light."

"You'll need more than words when you square off with The Beast," Warden Hess said. "You'll *have* to kill him to stop him."

"So you say," Remi replied.

"Well, kill him or not, you'd better win," Warden Hess said.

"And *you'd* better keep your word," Remi said. "If anything happens to Kundo, or if you don't give Eboni that antivirus, I won't fight another fight for you and I will kill you the first chance I get."

"If you weren't so valuable, you would not be allowed to speak to me this way."

"But I am, so…"

"For now," Warden Hess said.

The warden continued her massage. Her touch was a bit firmer now; a bit less gentle.

####

Remi glared across the cage at a mountain of a man who stood nearly twice her height. Stanley 'The Beast' Frank's thick, striated muscles shone under the stage lights that illuminated the ring. The giant pounded his barrel-like chest with his ham-sized fists, turning his peach-hued flesh deep praline. He pointed a thick finger at Remi and shouted "Sie werden nun neger sterben!" – *"Now you will die, nigger!"*

Remi pointed back at The Beast and replied "Atari wo orun mo o bi enipe ko ni ibe-e re." – *"The skull stares at heaven like it won't wind up there itself one day."*

The Beast's face twisted into a mask of rage. Remi knew he did not understand Yoruba like she understood German, but he knew she had retorted with more wit than his insult. Remi also knew that his rage was not normal; it was fueled by something else. Not AMVO; Peggy had admitted that every man who was infected with the AMVO virus had died, within days of initial infection, from a stroke – the already aggressive nature of men increased to astronomical levels by the virus, was too much for their brains to handle. *We're all just lab rats for these bastards,* Remi thought.

The Beast charged forward, crouching low in a classic wrestler's stance.

Remi leapt forward, rending the air with a powerful flying knee. Her knee slammed into The Beast's chin.

The Beast staggered backward, shaking his head as if to dislodge the pain in his rattled skull.

Remi unleashed a volley of punches to The Beast's body. It felt as if she was punching a stone statue.

The Beast grunted with each blow. He countered with a sweeping backhand slap.

Remi weaved under the slap and countered with a hook to The Beast's kidney.

The Beast dropped to one knee.

Remi shuffled around to The Beast's

back and reached for his neck with both hands.

Before Remi could wrap her arms around The Beast's neck and lock on a choke, however, the giant threw his body backward, slamming the back of his head into Remi's chest.

Remi flew backward, stopping only when her back crashed into the side of the cage.

The Beast spun on his knee and then sprang to his feet. He sprinted toward Remi as she sailed through the air.

Remi bounced off the cage and into The Beast's massive, open arms.

The Beast wrapped his forearms around her waist. He then arched his back as he snapped his arms upward.

Remi felt herself somersaulting over The Beast's head as his crushing grip on her waist increased, compressing her ribcage.

Remi landed on the floor of the cage with a loud thud.

The Beast landed on top of her, his chest crashing into hers.

Remi felt as if her ribcage had shrunk to a quarter of its normal breadth. Her liver, spleen and lungs felt as if a boulder had been dropped on them. Pain ripped through her torso.

The Beast threw his right leg over Remi's belly and straddled her. He drew back his right fist in preparation to strike.

Remi drove her hips upward, launching The Beast off-balance.

He fell forward, his chest shooting over Remi's head. He extended his hands to catch himself and prevent his face from slamming into the floor.

Remi reached up with both hands, trapping The Beast's left arm with both of her wrists. She then yanked her elbows down to her belly, pinning his arm against her chest.

The Beast yanked hard, struggling to free his arm, but both of Remi's arms against his one arm was too much and he couldn't break free from her grasp. She placed her right foot on the side of his left foot, trapping it as tightly as she held his left arm.

Remi thrust her hips upward once more, forcing The Beast's weight onto her lower torso. She then rolled to her right, throwing The Beast sideways.

The Beast landed on his back, with Remi kneeling between his legs. He crossed his ankles behind her back, trapping Remi between his legs.

Remi speared her left hand between The Beast's legs and then wrapped her arms around his right thigh, squeezing with all her might. She then hopped up onto the balls of her feet. Remi exploded upward into a standing position, thrusting her hips forward and into The Beast's buttocks.

The force of Remi's movement sent The Beast flying high into the air. Remi held him aloft for a moment and then drove her arms and her torso downward, snapping The Beast toward the floor.

The back of The Beast's skull

slammed into the floor. His arms flailed upward and his legs fell limply to the floor. He convulsed violently for a second and then was still.

Remi stood over The Beast, staring at his face, searching his dull, unfocused eyes for a sign of life. There was none. She then searched her heart for any remorse. There was none.

Jason Liu grabbed her wrist and raised her hand in victory. "The winner," he bellowed. "And new Grand Champion...Remi 'The Single Link' Swan!"

The spectators went wild.

Warden Hess entered the cage and slipped a heavy leather belt around her waist. The belt was decorated with several small gold plates with the names of each prison engraved on them and a large, circular, gold emblem of the state of Georgia at its center.

"Well done!" Warden Hess whispered in Remi's ear.

"Call in the order for Eboni to receive the anti-virus now!" Remi replied.

"And call off whoever you have waiting to harm my husband!"

"Already done on both accounts," Warden Hess said. "Now, let's get you to the van. I have a change of clothes waiting for you there."

"Okay," Remi said.

Warden Hess turned away from Remi and walked toward the cage door. "I'll see you back at Ames," Warden Hess said, peering over her shoulder. "Officers Dillard and Mc Cray are waiting at the bottom of the steps; they will lead you out of this madhouse and to the transport bay."

Remi nodded. Warden Hess exited the cage. Remi perused the faces in the stands. They were so happy. Money was made at the cost of the well-being and the lives of the fighters; the prisoners, who had been turned into savages and let loose upon each other. She vowed that she would tear it all down. That she would destroy the system, if it was the last thing she ever did.

ROUND FIVE

Remi spent the ride back to Ames praying that the Orisa Ogun use his mighty cutlass to chop down the towering tree of rage that sprouted from her mind; to sever the roots that crept down her spine and throughout her nervous system. She knew that if she fought in another tournament she would lose herself; she would give in to the rage, to the impulse to destroy and she would end up just like Janine. She was *not* going to let that be her fate.

When the van parked in the transport bay at Ames, Remi was helped down from the van by Officer McCray and then he and Officer Dillard escorted Remi to the infirmary.

"Why are we here?" Remi inquired.

"Warden Hess wants you to have x-rays done to insure all is okay," Officer Dillard replied. She also wants you to have a debriefing with Peggy."

"Okay," Remi said. "When will I get to see Eboni?"

"After our session," a familiar voice came from her right flank.

Remi turned toward the voice. Peggy rolled toward her.

"Remi," Peggy crooned. "Congratulations on your win!"

"Yeah, thanks," Remi replied. "So, do I see you first, or do we meet after the x-rays?"

"We can meet now," Peggy said, extending her hand toward Remi.

Remi stared at Peggy's hand for a moment and then shook it. A moment later, she felt a sharp pain in her thigh. She looked down. Peggy had jammed a needle into her quadriceps. Officers Dillard and McCray grabbed her arms and shoved them behind her back. She felt the bite of handcuffs tightening around her wrists.

"Why?" Remi croaked.

"I have something to show you and I can't have you freaking out in here when you see it," Peggy said.

Remi's legs buckled. The officers pulled up on her biceps to prevent her from falling.

Peggy turned away from Remi and began to roll away. "Bring her over here," she said over her shoulder.

Officers Dillard and McCray walked Remi over to a gurney that a body lay upon. The body was covered with a white sheet.

"No," Remi whispered. Her heart felt as if it was trying to punch its way out of her chest.

"It is important we start our discussion with transparency," Peggy said, grabbing the edge of the sheet that covered whatever lay on the gurney. "So, all questions will be answered; all will be revealed. I only sedated you because your response can't be predicted."

Peggy snatched the sheet from over the body on the gurney.

Remi stared down at Eboni's lifeless face. Her expression was peaceful. One corner of her mouth was upturned slightly. It was probably a sign she suffered a stroke, but knowing Eboni, it could have been her smirking as she said "I'm free, bastards, so screw you!"

Tears burst from beneath Remi's eyelids and rushed and rained down her face. "The antivirus...what happened?"

"There was no antivirus," Peggy replied. "There is no cure for however AMVO manifests in a patient. My apologies."

"It was a lie!" Remi felt her rage pumping the sedative out of her veins. "You knew Eboni was going to die, but you led me to believe she could be saved?"

"We needed you to win that tournament," Peggy said. "To prove that AMVO works."

"So, my winning wasn't about bragging rights, or money?"

"It was about that to a small degree," Peggy said. "Primarily, though, it is about creating a superior soldier; a superior human being."

Remi leaned forward and kissed Eboni on the cheek. "This is for you, sister," she whispered.

Remi thrust her right foot backward. Her heel slammed into Officer McCray's belly.

Officer McCray's waist folded around Remi's foot. A torrent of blood erupted from his mouth. His lifeless body fell to the floor with a wet thud.

Remi whirled to face Officer Dillard.

Officer Dillard back pedaled a few steps as he drew his shock baton.

Remi pulled against the handcuffs

with all her might. The chain snapped, freeing her hands. She wrapped her fingers around Peggy's neck and then snatched the woman out of her wheelchair.

"Please," Peggy cried. "I'm sorry! Please, don't!"

Remi hurled Peggy as if she was throwing a stone. Peggy crashed into Officer Dillard. They fell to the floor, with Peggy on top of Officer Dillard. Dillard's shock baton, wedged between them and damaged by their collision, crackled and flashed, releasing a massive burst of electricity. Officer Dillard and Peggy convulsed and salivated and then lay still.

The doctors and nurses in the infirmary ran toward the exit in a panic, but the panel that controlled the doors was at the nurse's station and in their panic, no one had released them.

Remi ran to the nurse's station. She perused it and found the panel. Each button on it corresponded to a door's number, except for one, which was marked 'Main'.

"Step away from that door, I will kill you all!" Remi shouted.

The medical staff shuffled away from the door and huddled in a corner to the right of it.

Remi unlocked all the doors to the infirmary's rooms. "Janine!" she screamed.

Janine shuffled out of her room, staring shyly at the floor.

"The people in here hurt you, Janine," Remi said. "They called you a monster. They locked you up in here. They killed your mama."

"M-mama?" Janine said, looking up at Remi.

"Yes," Remi replied. "They killed your mama and my best friend. They're bad people and I am going to make them pay. I'm going to hurt them. What are *you* going to do?"

"I-I hurt bad people, too," Janine said.

"No!" A doctor screamed.

Remi unlocked the exit door and then sprinted toward it.

Janine roared and then leapt forward. She landed before the huddle of infirmary staff. A nurse extended his arms toward Janine and pleaded for his life. Janine grabbed the man's wrists and then yanked both of his arms off with the ease a man tears a sheet of paper. Blood painted the walls.

Remi dashed out of the infirmary and into the hallway. She had a lot more work to do and the rage within her had grown into a maelstrom.

####

Remi drove the van out of the transport bay, past the gate's guards who she had beaten to death and out the open gate. It would take the authorities days to search through the carnage and discover she had escaped. If Janine was still at Ames when they came, she would kill them all. If she was at large, they would be busy hunting her. *Either way, I have time to get my family and get the hell out of Georgia*, she thought.

Remi was going home.

ROUND SIX

The twenty or so mile jog felt like a short jog around the block to Remi. Her strength, her endurance and her speed had grown exponentially. She now stood before her home. All the lights were off. The children – and probably Kundo – would be asleep.

She crept up the stairs. She patted her short afro and then ran her fingers across her eyebrows. She inspected her blood-stained white prison garments, patting them to remove any wrinkles and then rang the doorbell.

After a few moments, the door opened. Kundo stood before her, supporting himself with a cane.

"Remi?" Kundo gasped. "Baby?"

Tears streamed down Remi's face. No words would come from her lips, so she just nodded.

Kundo extended his free arm. Remi dashed inside, wrapping her arms around Kundo's waist. She pressed her head to his chest.

"What the hell happened?" Kundo said, closing the door.

"I couldn't take it in there any longer, Kundo," Remi replied.

"What have you done, Remi?" Kundo said, stepping back and gazing into her eyes.

"I did what I had to do to get out of there," Remi replied.

"How did you get here?"

"I drove halfway," Remi said. "I ditched the van back in Decatur and jogged the rest of the way."

"You jogged over twenty miles?" Kundo said.

"They did things to me in there, baby," Remi replied. "I've...changed. But tell me, what happened to you. They told me you were in a car accident."

"Yeah, an unmarked white van ran me off the road," Kundo said. "Killed the attorney Dan retained for y'all; left me with a broken right femur, four broken ribs a shattered collarbone and a severe concussion. I just came home three days ago. The children stayed with Dee."

"How *is* Dee?" Remi inquired.

"Crazy as ever," Kundo replied. "She's been running your classes since you've been gone."

"Good."

"Where's Eboni?" Kundo asked. "Did she escape with you?"

Remi lowered her gaze.

Kundo raised Remi's chin with his fingertips. "Remi? Where's Eboni?"

"She's dead, Kundo." Remi replied.

"What? No!" Kundo cried. "How?"

"They murdered her, Kundo," Remi replied. "We were infected with a virus they call AMVO. It changed me; it killed her."

"Who is 'they'?" Kundo said.

"The Warden and Medical staff at Ames," Remi said. "I don't know, could be the whole damn system."

"And you say they changed you? How?"

Remi yanked her top over her head and then tossed it onto the floor, revealing her hyper-defined, stone-hard muscles.

"What the hell?" Kundo gasped.

"I'm ten times stronger, faster and more enduring than I ever was," Remi said. "But I also have an aggression; a rage that frightens me."

Kundo shook his head. "I have never..."

"Mommy?"

Remi looked past Kundo towards the soft voice that interrupted him. Standing behind him was a plump toddler and a lean little boy.

"Ayo!" Remi said, opening her arms wide. "Tutu!"

The children ran past Kundo and leaped into Remi's arms.

"I missed you both so much," Remi sobbed.

Tutu wiped the tears from Remi's cheeks. "Don't cry mommy. Aren't you happy to see us?"

"Very happy," Remi replied. "Happier than I have ever been in my life!"

Ayo poked Remi's biceps with his finger. "Man, you have some hard muscles, mom! Harder than daddy's!"

Kundo rolled his eyes. "I've been out of commission since the accident, that's all."

"Your muscles were never this hard,

daddy!"

"Boy, it's still late, you're still sleepy," Kundo said. Now, let your mama get changed. You'll see her in the morning."

Remi chuckled.

"Okay," Ayo said. "See you in the morning, mom."

"See you later, mommy," Tutu said.

"See you in the morning, loves," Remi replied. "I love you!"

"We love you, too!" The children said in unison as they scampered off to bed.

"Come on," Kundo said. "Let's get you a hot bath and in some fresh clothes. We have a lot to discuss."

"And to do," Remi said, placing her hand on Kundo's chest.

"Kundo smiled. "Indeed!"

Dee took a sip of hot chai and then sat her cup on a saucer. "So, you mean to tell me all I needed to do was go to prison to get a body like that? Let me find a cop to beat up right now!"

"Dee!" Remi bellowed, shaking her head.

"I'm just sayin', girl!" Dee replied. "So, we gotta get you out of here before the police, or the FBI or whoever comes calling."

"Yeah, we have to find you a safe place to hide out," Kundo said. "The rest of us have to act like nothing has changed. They'll be watching all of our homes and hangouts."

"You know my aunt Charlotte?" Dee said. "The one I go check on during the day?"

"The blind and deaf one?" Remi said.

"Yeah," Dee replied. "She has a fixed basement. You can stay down there. We can sneak you in. No one will be the wiser."

"Doesn't she have a nurse who stays

there overnight?" Remi asked.

"She's *supposed* to be there overnight," Dee replied. "But as soon as Aunt Charlotte goes to sleep around nine, Little Miss Florence Nightingale is out the door to go lay up under her boyfriend."

"So, let's get you some clothes packed and head out while the children are at school," Kundo said. "We don't want them crying for their iya."

"What are you going to tell them?" Remi inquired. "I just got home last night and I'm leaving them again."

"We probably have another day or two before they start surveillance on all of us," Kundo replied. "I'll bring them by tonight...maybe tomorrow, too."

"Has anyone checked the news?" Dee asked. "Any word about Ames, Remi or Eboni?"

"When I was dropping off the children at school, there was mention in the news about a rabid bear attacking people in Cobb County," Kundo replied. "About five or six miles from where Ames is located."

"Janine," Remi said.

"Probably," Kundo said. "They said State Police put the 'bear' down."

"They're covering up what happened," Remi said. "I left a mess back there. I'm sure Janine did much worse. They'll find Eboni's body and figure I'm dead, too. It'll take a while for them to figure out I'm not."

"Good!" Dee said. "Come on y'all; let's get you settled in at Aunt Charlotte's. My stories are about to come on!"

Aunt Charlotte's basement was cozy. The sky blue walls were covered with velvet black light posters – a nude couple with huge afros embracing and kissing each other; a spear and rifle-wielding Huey P. Newton sitting in a wicker chair; Imaro, the 'African Conan', pointing a sword skyward, with an axe-wielding sister kneeling beside him – remnants of a time when Aunt Charlotte was a Professor of African History and active in the Black

Arts Movement. The basement was sparsely furnished with a black leather couch, loveseat and chair suite and an old 27" television.

Kundo sat a duffle bag next to the television. "It's nice down here," Kundo said. "You should be..." His words were halted by a fit of coughing. Beads of sweat formed on his forehead and the tip of his nose.

"Baby, are you okay?" Remi said.

"I'm okay," Kundo whispered. "Not feeling too good. Probably the flu trying to come on; I'll stop by Ajigunwa's shop on the way home and get some golden seal."

"Okay," Remi said. "Be sure to take care of it. I need you strong in case we have to run."

"I'll be re..." more coughing. Kundo cane fell from his fist. He staggered backward.

"Take a seat, Kundo," Remi said, lunging toward him.

Kundo plopped down on the couch.

Remi placed her hand on his shoulder. His shirt was soaked with sweat.

"Are you okay, Kundo?" Dee whispered as she crept down the stairs with a blanket, pillow and sheet cradled in her arms.

Kundo coughed again.

"He's not feeling well," Remi replied. "Did the nurse hear him coughing?"

"Girl, she's up there watching the stories with me," Dee said. "I got the t.v. up loud, so she can't hear anything."

"Good," Kundo said. "I don't know what's wrong with me. I woke up with a slight headache and now I feel lightheaded and my chest hurts."

"Here, girl," Dee said, extending her arms toward Remi. "Take these covers, so I can get back in there before she comes checking up on me. I'll give her the rest of the day off."

Remi took the covers and pillow from Dee and then laid them on the loveseat. "Can you pick up Ayo and Tutu from school for us? Kundo needs to rest."

"I got you, girl," Dee said. "I'll drop the children off here. You think you're gonna be okay to take them to school in the morning, Kundo? Lord knows, their bad butts aren't gonna be quiet down here."

You got that right," Kundo chuckled. "I should be fine in a minute. Do us one more favor and pick up some golden seal from Ajigunwa's so I can make me some tea, please?"

"I'm gonna have to start charging y'all for all these favors," Dee said.

"We pay you in love, Dee," Kundo replied. "Money can't buy happiness."

Dee sucked her teeth. "Love don't pay the rent; and money might not bring you happiness, but it can sho' help you be miserable in comfort."

Kundo and Remi laughed.

"See," Kundo said. "Crazy as ever."

Remi nodded in agreement.

"I'll be back down after she leaves," Dee said. "And after my stories." Dee turned and crept back upstairs.

Remi sat beside Kundo and laid her head on his shoulder. "I think I know why you're sick, Kundo."

"Why do you think?" Kundo replied.

"It's AMVO," Remi said. "When we made love last night, I infected you."

"You can't be sure of that," Kundo said. "It's probably just a coincidence."

"You never get sick," Remi replied. "And I, like the Creator, do not play with dice and do not believe in coincidence."

"Not much I can do if I *am* infected," Kundo said. "I'm not..."

Kundo fell over onto the arm of the couch.

Remi sat bolt upright. "Kundo?" she gasped. He didn't respond.

She studied his face. His eyes were closed and one corner of his mouth was turned upward in a slight smile...like

Eboni's. Remi shook Kundo's shoulders. "Baby? Baby, wake up!"

Kundo moaned. Remi breathed a sigh of relief.

"You're a warrior, Kundo," Remi said, holding Kundo's head in her lap. "You taught me to never quit; to fight until my last breath. Don't be a hypocrite! You fight...you hear me? Fight!"

####

Kundo's eyes fluttered open. Remi was looking down at him. She gave him a smile.

"Good morning, sunshine," she said.

"Finally up, huh, Rip Van Winkle?" Dee said.

"How long was I out?" Kundo asked.

"A long time," Dee said. "The children are over there asleep and Aunt Charlotte is in bed already."

"What?" Kundo said, sitting up. He followed Dee's finger. Ayo and Tutu were fast asleep on a blanket in front of the television.

"How do you feel?" Remi asked.

"Strong," Kundo replied.

"Take off your top," Remi said.

"Hey, wait until I leave, lovebirds," Dee said.

"I don't want him to strip for me," Remi said shaking her head. "I need to see something. Baby, please, take off your dashiki."

Kundo slipped the dashiki over his head, revealing his rock hard physique.

"Look," Remi said, pointing at Kundo's torso.

"Dang, Kundo," Dee said. "You look like you just lost the little bit of body fat you had in a few hours."

"And your injuries," Remi said. "How do they feel?"

Kundo stood up. He shook his arms and legs. "I...I don't feel them."

"It's the AMVO," Remi said.

"So, your blood can heal," Kundo said. "It can enhance physical attributes."

"Girl, you a doggone superhero!" Dee said. "I'm gonna have to turn vampire and get some of your blood, shoot!"

"That's a good idea," Remi said.

"What?" Dee said, frowning. "Girl, I was just kidding. Shoot, I don't even drink wine at communion. I ain't drinkin' your blood!"

"No, not you," Remi said. "But if my blood can do this for Kundo, it can do it for others. We can raise an army."

"For what purpose?" Kundo asked.

"To bring down the system that made me this way in the first place," Remi replied. "To put an end to the corporate slavery they call the penal system."

"Let me get this straight," Kundo said. "You want to infect other warriors with AMVO to create an army of super soldiers that will topple this corrupt ass slave state?"

"Yes," Remi replied. She lowered her gaze. "I know it sounds crazy, but..."

"That's my baby!" Kundo said. "That's brilliant!"

"My friends have lost their minds," Dee sighed.

"Maybe we have," Remi said. "You in?"

"Of course," Dee replied. "Somebody with some sense has gotta be in this to balance y'all out."

"Whoot-whoot," Remi said, wrapping her arms around Dee.

"But I'm not drinking no blood," Dee said. "Y'all can be Superman and Superwoman...I'll be Rorschach or the Bat. If I come home all ripped, my husband is gonna have some serious questions."

"Isn't he on a run to Chicago?" Kundo inquired.

"Yeah, thank God," Dee said. "The last thing I need is for him to be asking me a bunch of questions."

"Is Dan back?" Remi asked.

"He got back early this morning," Kundo replied.

"You think you can convince him to bankroll this operation?" Remi said. "I know he's all about the money and he won't be making anything from this; only giving."

"Dan will do it," Kundo replied. "He'll do it because he's my best friend; my brother... and because there is *always* profit in war."

Dan Wallace, the CEO of World Extreme Ring Kombat – or WERK – the organization that gave Remi her shot at being the first woman to fight men in professional MMA matches, walked down the stairs to Aunt Charlotte's basement, led by Dee.

Kundo beamed when he saw him. "Dan!"

Dan bounded down the stairs and ran to his friend. The men hugged.

"Man, you said you were still in pain from the accident and that you felt sick this morning," Dan said. "You look better than ever. Were you taking the piss?"

"Eww," Dee said, turning up her nose.

"No, not taking *a* piss, love," Dan said. "Taking *the* piss. In England, we say you're 'taking the piss' if you're teasing someone."

"Oh," Dee said. "Thanks, for clarifying that."

"No, I wasn't teasing," Kundo said.

"It's a miracle, then?" Dan said with a smirk.

"Of sorts," Kundo replied. He peered over his shoulder toward the bathroom door behind him. "Come on out, baby!" he called.

Remi sauntered out of the bathroom.

"What the hell?" Dan gasped. "When...how did you get out?"

"Have a seat, brother," Kundo said. "We have a lot to tell you."

####

"And you want me to believe you have super powers?" Dan said, shaking his head.

"Not super," Kundo said. "Not powers, either. *Enhanced Abilities*, is what we prefer to call it."

"I find this impossible to believe," Dan said.

"You can see the difference in our bodies," Remi said.

"You're definitely more muscular; more defined," Dan replied. "But ten times stronger? Ten times as quick? That is not possible!"

"I'm nowhere near as enhanced as Remi," Kundo said. "I'm maybe a bit beyond the upper limits of human physical ability."

"No, sir," Dan said, shaking his head.

We'll just have to show you," Remi said. "Stand up."

"Uh oh," Dee said. "Somebody's about to get whooped."

"Remi," Dan crooned. "You don't want none."

"Oh, I do," Remi said smiling.

"She does," Kundo said.

Dan stood and then removed his suit jacket. "I won't hold back."

"Don't," Remi replied.

"Alright, then," Dan said. He inhaled deeply. A moment later, he tossed his jacket toward Remi's face and then darted behind it.

Remi lunged sideways, evading the jacket. She thrust her knee upward, driving it into Dan's thigh.

The force of the blow sent Dan somersaulting forward. His back crashed onto the floor.

Remi grabbed his belt and yanked him off the floor. She held Dan above her head. "Convinced now?" she asked, staring up into his quivering face.

"Y-yeah," Dan said. "I-I'm convinced!"

Remi sat Dan down on the loveseat.

"Want some tea, child?" Dee snickered.

"Yes, thanks," Dan said. "Add some whiskey to that, please. I need a stiff drink."

"We're ready to bring it all down, Dan," Kundo said. "To finish what Nat Turner, Boukman Dutty, Three Fingered Jack, Nwanyeruwa, Blanca Canales and The Black Liberation Army started, like we used to talk about back in college."

"I'm with you," Dan said. "But nobody in their right minds is going to allow themselves to be infected with *any*thing, let alone a virus that changes them so radically."

"Then we need people *not* in their right minds," Remi said. "People who would do anything to see their people free."

"Hmm...I can't guarantee anything, but I might know just the people," Dan said.

"Who?" Kundo asked.

"Your boy, Changa bin Wahad and his Freedom Takes Power brothers and sisters," Dan replied.

"Man, they might be *too* crazy," Kundo said, shaking his head. "Changa bin Wahad once said in a lecture that the best he can hope for is to die in a pose that confuses future archaeologists."

Remi laughed. "Sounds like *exactly* who we need with us! Hook it up, y'all!"

"Okay," Dan said. "Kundo, come with me. FTP respects you. And I know that Changa and some of his people were at your fight against Chris Cunningham, Remi."

"Alright, Remi," Kundo said. "If we

meet with Changa and all goes well, you'll have your army."

"Good luck," Changa bin Wahad called from the balcony, upon which he and his crew stood.

Kundo and Remi dropped to one knee, raising their left hand to their forehead as they pressed their right fist to the floor in salutation to Changa and five of his closest comrades in the FTP Movement – Ogunbala, his Chief-Of-Security; Mecca Asiatic, his wife and Co-Chairperson; Fang Sing, a rapper, artist and martial arts expert, turned activist; and the twins Akin and Koya, both professors at Spelman College and revolutionaries. The warriors of FTP pounded their chests with their fists in a show of mutual respect.

They met in a warehouse Dan purchased decades ago; a place where he held underground fights before going legit. Tonight, this place, where much blood was spilled and where men and women proved their skill in combat, would once again be

126

a place where warriors would prove their mettle, or die trying.

Dan, who stood beside Changa bin Wahad, held a device in his hand that looked like an oversized remote control. He waved it about as he spoke. "The brothers and sisters of FTP are willing to join your cause if what you say you can do is real. They require...no they *demand* a demonstration. Are you ready?"

Remi and Kundo sprang to their feet. "Ready!" They said in unison.

"Then let the demonstration begin!" Dan said, pressing a button on the remote.

Two loud clicking sounds followed, as if large locks had come undone. A moment later, a sound, like distance thunder, echoed throughout the warehouse. A huge grizzly bear galloped into view.

"Oh, damn," Changa gasped. "Brother, what is this? I didn't come here to see this brother and sister get slaughtered."

"Just watch, please," Dan replied.

"And where in the hell did you get a grizzly bear?" Changa said, shaking his head. "I guess money *can* buy anything."

"I'm renting, actually," Dan replied. "They aren't allowed to kill the bear; just subdue it."

The grizzly bear stood on its hind legs and then roared, baring its dagger-like teeth and claws.

Kundo stomped at the bear. "Come on!"

The bear charged. Kundo rushed to meet it, running at blinding speed. He leapt over the bear's head, punching downward into the top of its skull as it passed under him.

The bear stopped charging. It grunted as it shook its massive head. The bear stood again, turned and lumbered toward Kundo.

Kundo jumped into the air, twisting his hips until his back was toward the creature. He then thrust his foot behind him, striking the bear in the belly with a powerful back kick.

The bear stumbled backward, roaring in protest.

Remi dug her fingers into the fur at the bear's lower back. She thrust her hips forward and then raised her arms above her head, jerkking the bear off its feet.

The bear howled in fear.

Remi arched backward, snatching the bear over her head and then slamming its shoulders onto the concrete floor.

The bear's back hit with a booming din. The creature curled up into an unmoving heap.

The members of FTP stood in stunned silence, their eyes as wide as dinner plates.

After a long pause, Changa bin Wahad spoke. "Sign...me...*up!*"

"Did you kill my bear?" Dan asked, wagging his finger.

"It's still alive," Kundo replied. "Out

like a light, though."

"Come on down," Remi said. "Dee and I prepared dinner; let's discuss our next move over some good food."

####

The members of FTP sat on one side of a long table, devouring the black bean enchiladas, curried couscous and eggplant parmesan. Remi, Kundo, Dee and Dan sat on the other side.

"This food is delicious," Changa said. "My compliments to the chefs."

"Thank you," Dee said.

"Thanks," Remi replied. "There's honey bean pie for dessert. Kundo told me it is one of your favorites."

One of my favorites?" Changa said. "Honey bean pie should be one of the food groups!"

"So, what's the plan?" Mecca Asiatic asked.

"We're going to break into two women's prisons," Remi replied. "Pulaski, in Hawkensville and Arrondale, in Habersham County. We're going to set all the women free and then burn the prisons to the ground. We'll hit Pulaski first and then Arrondale three hours later."

"And then?" Mecca said.

"Then we flood social media with videos and tweets admitting we did it and why," Remi said. "We explain to the world that since the very nature of the prison system requires brutality and contempt for the people imprisoned, it cannot be reformed."

"I feel you on that, sister," Mecca replied.

"We call for the abolishment of all prisons," Remi said. "And we give our word that *we* will police our communities and train others to do the same."

"So, we're about to be the world's first superheroes is what you're saying," Changa chimed in.

"I...I guess so, yeah," Remi replied.

"Then, we need a name," Changa

said. "Every superhero team has a name."

"Like the Revengers, or the X-Klan, or somethin'?" Fang Sing asked.

"Nah, not that white-bread, bang pow, zoink ish," Changa replied. "I'm thinking...'The Siafu'."

"The Siafu?" Remi echoed. "Explain."

"The Siafu are African ants," Changa replied. "They have no eyes, no venom...only strong jaws. Individually, each Siafu is small, but as a team, they can strip a water buffalo down to the bone in less than an hour."

"Damn," Kundo said.

"We are much like the Siafu Ant," Changa said. "Small in size; small in numbers, but powerful beyond measure."

"Siafu, it is, then," Remi said.

"So, when do we receive our superpowers?" Changa asked.

Remi nodded toward Changa's empty plate. "You already have."

ROUND SEVEN

Kundo and Changa inspected the crew, who stood in a single rank before a black Chevy Suburban SUV. All of them were dressed in black, cotton jumpsuits with a mock turtleneck underneath; black tactical boots and a black ski mask atop their heads.

"Tighten the straps on your vests," Kundo said, tugging at the shoulder and side straps of his bulletproof vest in demonstration. The rest of them followed suit.

"Looking good, Siafu!" Remi said as she walked out of a room to their flank.

Kundo whistled. "Looking good

yourself, baby!"

"You think so?" Remi said, whirling on her heels. She wore a quilted, oxblood leather jacket with matching trousers, boots and fingerless driving gloves.

"I *know* so," Kundo replied.

"So how do y'all feel?" Remi asked the group.

"Well, today, for the first time in many years, I was able to carry Mecca across the threshold of our hotel room," Changa snickered.

Mecca sucked her teeth. "Very funny."

"Thanks for the luxurious digs, last night, too," Changa said, nodding toward Dan.

"My pleasure," Dan replied. "It may be a while before we get to enjoy such luxuries again anytime soon, so I figured 'why not'?"

"And did Dee and your wife make it on the train with the children okay?" Remi asked.

"Yes," Dan answered. "I purchased three bedroom suites, which is more than enough room for the sisters and the babies. They'll meet us in Tallahassee."

"My folks will take care of them down there," Changa said. "If things go south, they're already set to take the fam' to Havana."

"I guess we're all set, then," Remi said. "Let's roll out!"

"Hello, everyone. I'm Danielle Pace – along with Quinton Williams, Barb Blake, Eric Rollins and Greg Adams. It's 5 o'clock in Atlanta and this is '*The Five at five*'."

Popular newscaster, Danielle Pace and her equally renowned co-hosts of the long-running, nightly news commentary sat at the mahogany roundtable dressed in their customary blue business suits.

"The Siafu has hit Arrendale State Women's Prison, just three hours after striking at Pulaski Women's Prison in

Hawkensville, Georgia. They have left in their wake rivers of blood, charred flesh and smoldering embers."

A video popped up behind Danielle. The violence was pixilated to spare squeamish viewers and to keep the censors at bay.

"The terror network has released another barbaric video that appears to show a guard at Arrendale literally being torn apart by what appears to be a woman who is dressed from head to toe in dark red leather clothing like some comic book super-villain. The tape comes shortly after one in which The Siafu beheaded the warden of Pulaski Prison and committed other atrocities. White House Chief Intelligence Correspondent, Kate Hearn has seen both videos and she joins us now. Kate, can you tell us about today's events?"

A woman with fire red lipstick, in sharp contrast to her porcelain-colored skin, appeared on a screen over Danielle's shoulder.

"Well, thank you, Danielle. This five

minute-long video is particularly horrific because you see the guard sort of grab his skull in pain and the screams are sort of very...base; a primal scream of anger as he sort of collapses to his knees. So, this is meant to incite and to send a message to all watching that this Siafu group has declared war on the American citizens, Danielle."

"We appreciate that you watched the videos and bear witness to them for those of us who didn't watch them," Danielle replied. "We do, indeed, appreciate that. Greg, you have a question?"

"Yeah," Greg Adams said, shaking his head. "What does this say about the fruitlessness of negotiating, when they were...they were...I'm sorry; this is just too sickening..."

"Come on now," Eric Rollins chimed in with a smirk. "I mean, people tearing human beings to shreds like tissue paper? Come on. This is obviously some kind of sham to jerk us around!"

"Look, The Siafu is playing chess, not checkers," Kate replied. "They have carefully executed and managed this whole event.

Danielle turned her gaze toward a rotund Black man to her left. "Quinton?"

"So Kate," Quinton Williams began. "You say The Siafu have obviously declared war on America. What do you anticipate the next step of the President will be? Do you believe that he will call in the Armed Forces on this?"

"Well, there are multiple media sources coming out that indicate The Siafu might even be a violent arm of Al-Qaeda," Kate replied. "And may even be the ones who orchestrated the tragic fall of the Twin Towers way back in September 11, 2001. Remember that?"

"Kate, I've seen the prior video," Eric Rollins said. "I happened not to see this one. I understand this one ends with The Siafu burying a victim *inside* another victim."

"That's correct," Kate said.

"How are they pulling off these monstrous acts?" Eric said. "Is it CGI?

Camera tricks?"

"It's real," Kate replied. "We figure they must all be hopped up on PCP...and probably some powerful kind of steroid."

Barb Blake, the oldest of *The Five at five*, spoke. "So, where do you predict The Siafu will strike next, Kate?"

"Since they have hit two women's prisons, it is likely they will hit the next closest one, Julia Tutwiler Prison for Women in Wetumpka, Alabama," Kate answered.

"I know I have to let you go," Danielle said. "But can I ask you one last question, Kate, because I'm going to take the opposite...wait...what was that?"

Kate's eyes widened. Her jaw fell slack and her chin descended to her chest. "Oh, my God! It's...it's The Siafu! Lock those goddamned doors! Lock..."

Beeeeeeeeeeeep.

Remi appeared on television screens throughout Metropolitan Atlanta and its neighboring suburbs. The lower half of her face was concealed by a spiked, oxblood leather mask.

"Good evening, Atlanta, she began. Allow me first to apologize. I, like you, enjoy the science fiction and fantasy we call 'the news'; the laughs evoked by the shucking and jiving in our favorite comedy; the tranquility of a mind-numbing rap video. But in the spirit of our magnificent African History and our history throughout the Diaspora, we – The Siafu – thought we could take this time to honor our revolutionary ancestors, who, sadly, are no longer remembered. So, sit down and let's have a little chat before those who don't want us to speak come busting in with guns blazing and attempt to shut us down."

Remi shrugged her shoulders and extended her upturned palms.

"And shut us down, why? Because they know that while the flesh may die at the hands of the enforcers of this brutal, suffocating and oppressive system, revolution lives on forever. Revolution snatches the covers off of deception. It consumes lies in a raging flame, leaving only truth to rise from its ashes. And the truth is there's something horribly wrong with the United *Snakes* of America."

Remi shook her gloved fist at the camera.

"Savagery and corruption, racism and tyranny. COINTELPRO and MK-ULTRA were never abolished and we now accept every perversion and vice as part and parcel of the American Way. How did this happen? Who's responsible? You don't have to search too far. Just go in your bathroom and stare long and hard at your own reflection."

Remi shook her head.

"I know; I know. You were scared. Who wouldn't be? War; infectious, fatal disease; police shooting us down like dogs in the street. Fear got the best of you. Fear robbed you of your reason and your common sense. We were made to fear from the time we were babies. But why do we fear, now, since we are big men and women? We – and I am talking to *you*, Black man and woman, are, as a people, very afraid of this white man and his System. Why won't we stand up as a people for what is right and just? It is because we suffer from the burden of Fear. As babies, we drank "the milk of fear" from our mothers' breasts. "Fear" produces a hormonal or chemical reaction in the breast from the brain. When a woman is made afraid of what would happen to her or her child, or is subjected to a circumstance that produces "fear" and "insecurity," this, then, is bred into us!"

Remi leapt from her seat and then paced back and forth. Dan Wallace, who operated the commandeered camera, followed her with it.

"But we, The Siafu are here today to offer you something besides fear to drink. We are here to offer you the fear drenching waters of revolution. We are going to show you that the only way to conquer your fear is to conquer that which you fear."

Behind her, a video of Siafu ants, migrating across a tropical rainforest in Gabon, faded into view.

"So, join us, The Siafu...the tiny

ants that, together, can bring down an elephant. We Africans are always *in* war, but never *at* war. But right here; right now and until we *all* get free...the war is on!"

Beeeeeeeeep.

ABOUT THE AUTHOR

Balogun is the author of the bestselling *Afrikan Martial Arts: Discovering the Warrior Within* and screenwriter / producer / director of the films, *A Single Link, Rite of Passage: Initiation* and *Rite of Passage: The Dentist of Westminster.*

He is one of the leading authorities on Steamfunk – a philosophy or style of writing that combines the African and / or African American culture and approach to life with that of the steampunk philosophy and / or steampunk fiction – and writes about it, the craft of writing, Sword & Soul and Steampunk in general, at http://chroniclesofharriet.com/.

He is author of seven novels – the Steamfunk bestseller, *MOSES: The Chronicles of Harriet Tubman (Books 1 & 2)*; the Urban Science Fiction saga, *Redeemer*; the Sword & Soul epic, *Once Upon A Time In Afrika*, two Fight Fiction, New Pulp novellas – *A Single Link* and *Fist of Afrika*, the two-fisted Dieselfunk tale, *The Scythe* and the "Choose-Your-Own-

Destiny"-style Young Adult novel, *The Keys*. Balogun is also contributing co-editor of two anthologies: *Ki: Khanga: The Anthology* and *Steamfunk*.

Finally, Balogun is the Director and Fight Choreographer of the Steamfunk feature film, *Rite of Passage*, which he wrote based on the short story, *Rite of Passage*, by author Milton Davis and co-author of the award winning screenplay, *Ngolo*.

You can reach him on Facebook at www.facebook.com/Afrikan.Martial.Arts; on Twitter @Baba_Balogun and on Tumblr at www.tumblr.com/blog/blackspeculativefiction.

www.ingramcontent.com/pod-product-compliance
Lightning Source LLC
Chambersburg PA
CBHW070932130626
46555CB00001B/403